Y0-AXA-952

LEE COUNTY LIBRARY
107 HAWKINS AVE.
SANFORD, N. C. 27330

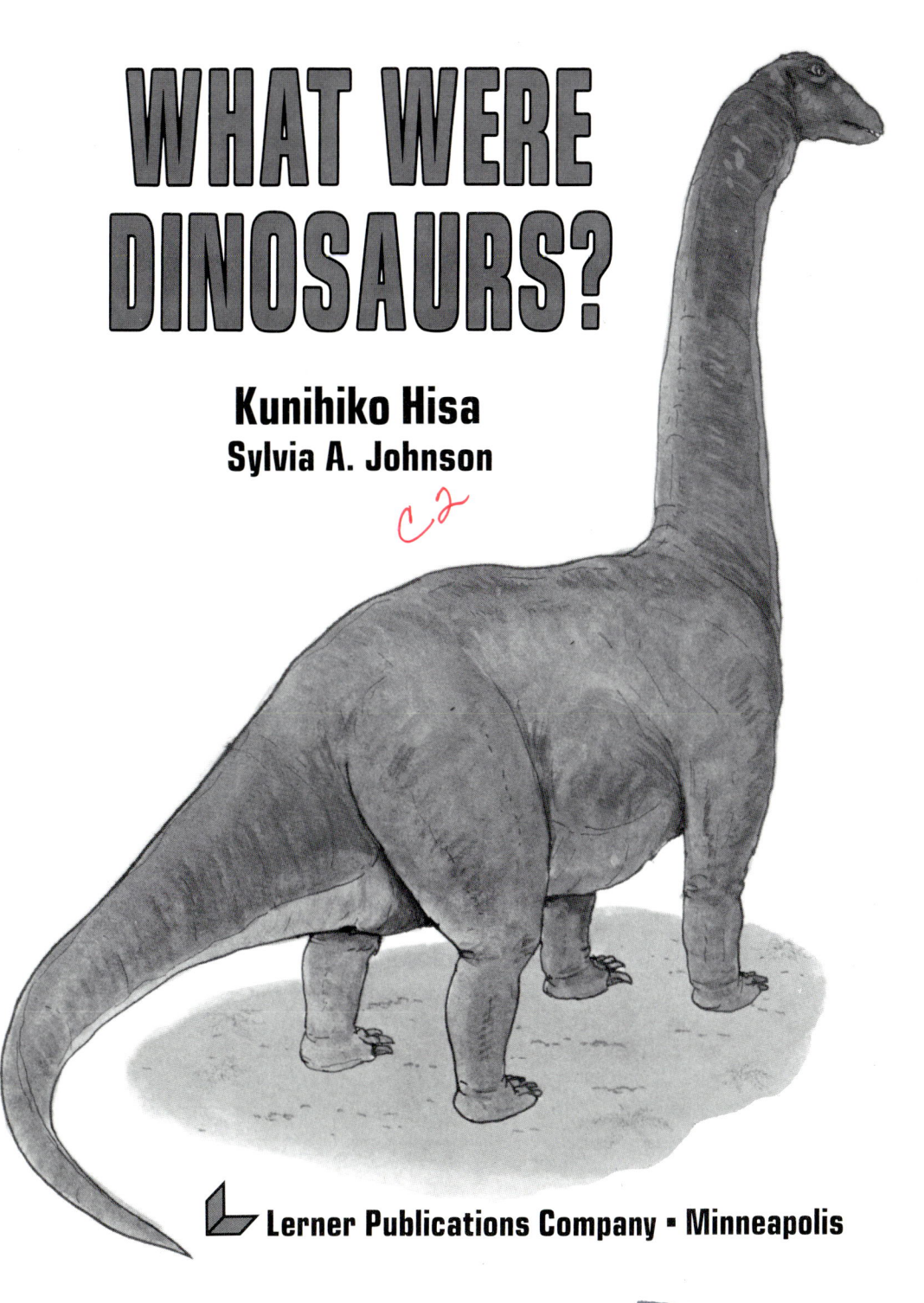

WHAT WERE DINOSAURS?

Kunihiko Hisa
Sylvia A. Johnson

Lerner Publications Company • Minneapolis

What Were Dinosaurs?

That's an easy question to answer. Everyone knows what dinosaurs were. They were giant reptiles, slow-moving and not too smart. Dinosaurs lived on earth a long time ago and then died out suddenly and completely, leaving behind only traces of their existence.

Brachiosaurus

Mamenchisaurus

Diplodocus

Polacanthus

Kentrosaurus

If this is your idea of what dinosaurs were, you might be in for some surprises. We know a lot more about dinosaurs now than we used to, and some of our new discoveries have changed such old, familiar ideas. There are also new ways of thinking about dinosaurs that have given us a better understanding of how these ancient animals lived.

Let's take a closer look at some dinosaurs and see if we can find out what they were really like.

Camarasaurus

Apatosaurus

Stegosaurus

When dinosaur remains were first discovered in the 1800s, people did not know what kind of strange animals the bones came from.

No Eyewitnesses

In trying to discover what dinosaurs were like, we have to keep in mind one important fact. No human being has ever seen a dinosaur in the flesh. Dinosaurs lived on earth millions of years before the first humans came into existence. Our knowledge of these fascinating animals is not based on the reports of eyewitnesses

4

or on photographs of living dinosaurs. It comes from a different kind of evidence.

It was not until the 1800s that people even knew dinosaurs had once walked the earth. During this century, dinosaurs bones were found in different places around the world. These ancient bones had been turned to stone by natural processes. Their discovery proved that some kind of strange animals had once lived on our planet. But what was the story that the bones told? What did the animals look like, and how did they live? These are questions that we are still trying to answer today.

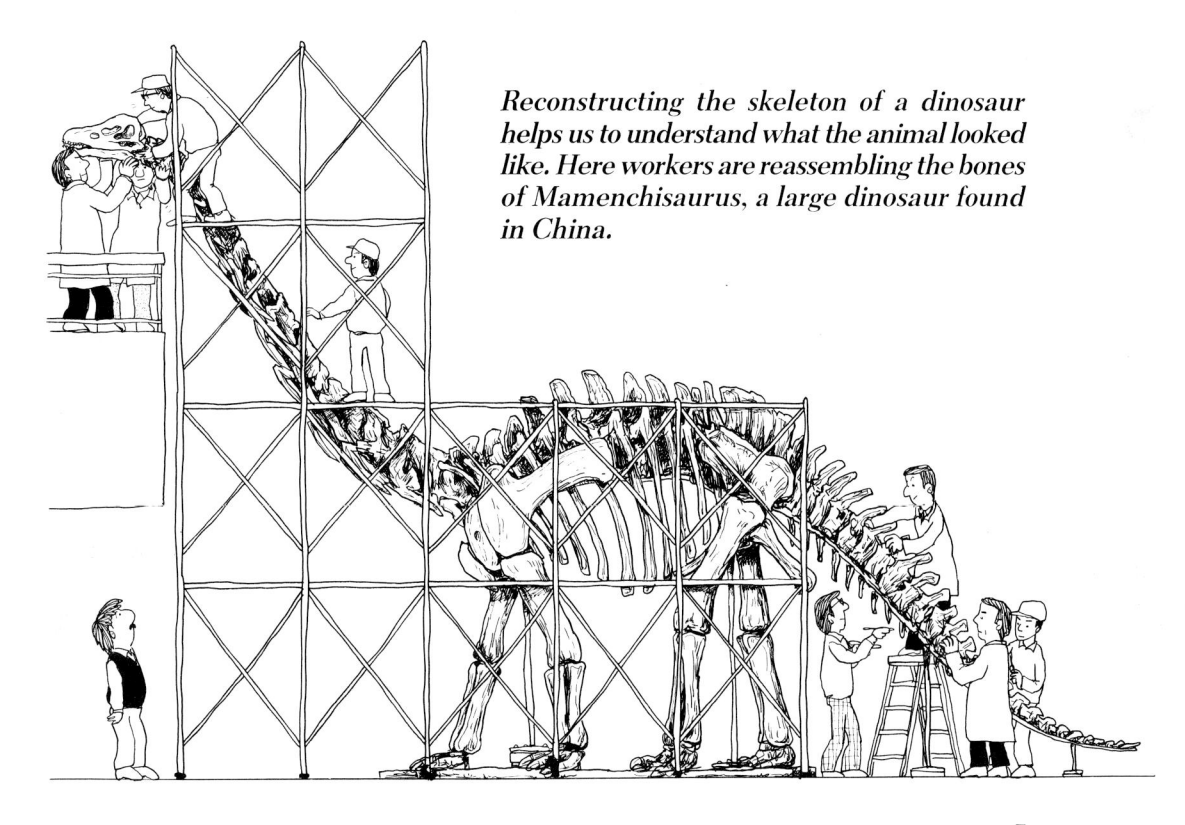

Reconstructing the skeleton of a dinosaur helps us to understand what the animal looked like. Here workers are reassembling the bones of Mamenchisaurus, a large dinosaur found in China.

Rhamphorhynchus
Jurassic period

Tyrannosaurus
Cretaceous period

Triceratops
Cretaceous period

Ankylosaurus
Cretaceous period

This illustration shows some familiar dinosaurs, along with one of their flying relatives, a pterosaur. These animals lived during different periods in the past, but here they are shown together in one imaginary scene. The artist also had to use imagination in deciding exactly how to picture the dinosaurs. What kind of information did he use in making his drawing?

Apatosaurus
Jurassic period

Stegosaurus
Jurassic period

Parasaurolophus
Cretaceous period

After an animal dies, its soft body parts decay. If its bones become buried under layers of mud or sand, they may eventually be preserved as fossils.

Fossil Evidence

What we know about dinosaurs is based on the evidence of *fossils* found buried in the earth. Fossils are records of ancient animals and plants that have been preserved over time. Most of the dinosaur fossils we have found are the remains of hard parts of the animals, such as bones and teeth. These body parts have been preserved because minerals have filled the small air spaces in them, turning them into stone. Soft body parts do not usually survive because they decay or are destroyed before the fossilizing process can take place.

Fossils can be useful pieces of evidence, but they do not tell a very complete story about ancient animals. One problem is that we do not often find the fossil remains of an entire animal. Even when all the bones of a dinosaur are preserved, they are not usually found joined together. Someone has to decide how the bones should be arranged to make a whole animal.

Another problem with fossil evidence is that it may tell us a very one-sided story about the animals of the past. Bones are preserved only if an animal dies under very special kinds of conditions. Millions of dinosaurs disappeared completely, without leaving any signs of their existence. When we try to imagine what ancient animals were like, we have to realize that we are missing many important pieces of evidence.

It would be easier to know what a dinosaur was like if its fossil remains were found neatly assembled. Since fossils are usually scattered, someone must decide how all the pieces fit together.

"*Because sauropods were such big, heavy animals, they needed water to support their bodies. With nostrils on top of their heads, they could breathe while submerged.*"

Because fossil evidence is so incomplete, it is not easy to decide what individual dinosaurs were like or how they lived. *Paleontologists* (scientists who study fossils) have often disagreed about what fossilized bones tell us. For example, in studying the bones of the large dinosaurs known as sauropods, these experts have come to very different conclusions. Some paleontologists believe that sauropods spent most of their time in water, while others insist that they were land animals.

"Sauropods had heavy leg bones and strong skeletons, like elephants. They must have lived on land."

Would you know what a cow's head looked like if you had only the skull?

Incorrect restoration   *Correct restoration*

Guesses and Deductions

To get an idea of the problems that paleontologists face in studying dinosaurs, imagine what it would be like to try and reconstruct modern animals only from their bones. Bones might tell you an animal's general shape, if you put them together correctly. But what about the muscle and tissue that covered the bones? Could you figure out how much of this soft material there should be and how it should be arranged? Just a small mistake in guessing here could produce an animal that looks very different from the real thing. And what about internal organs? Could you tell from looking at a cow's bones that the animal had a stomach with four different chambers?

Another part of an animal that is difficult to reconstruct is the covering of its body. What kind of skin or hide did it have? Was it covered with hair or scales or even feathers? What colors or patterns appeared on its body? Sometimes there are fossil clues to body coverings, but often guesswork and deduction are the only methods that can be used to complete the picture.

A skeleton gives no clues about the covering of an animal's body. What kind of hair or hide would you give this horse?

A horse with long, shaggy hair

A horse with a spotted hide

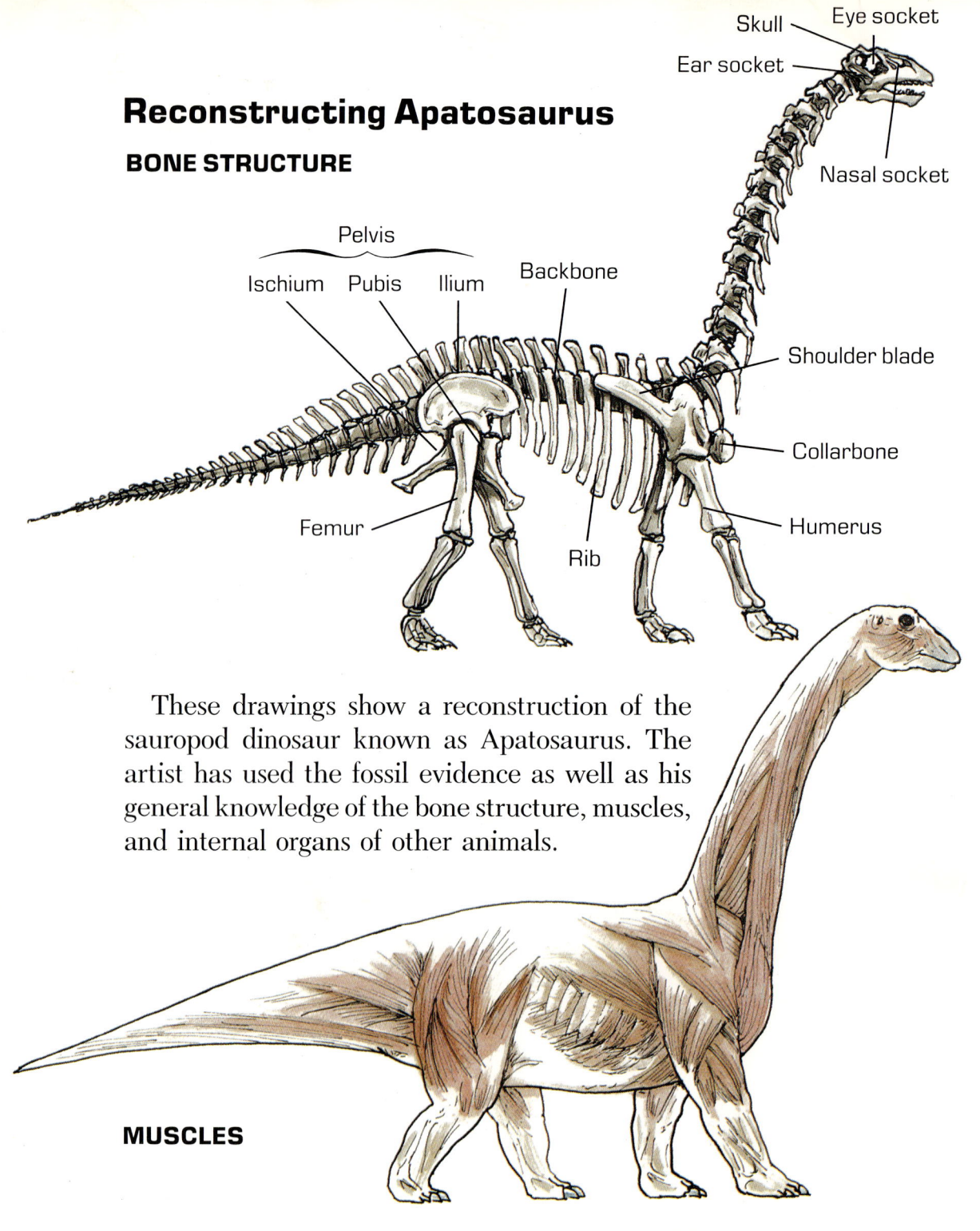

Reconstructing Apatosaurus

BONE STRUCTURE

These drawings show a reconstruction of the sauropod dinosaur known as Apatosaurus. The artist has used the fossil evidence as well as his general knowledge of the bone structure, muscles, and internal organs of other animals.

MUSCLES

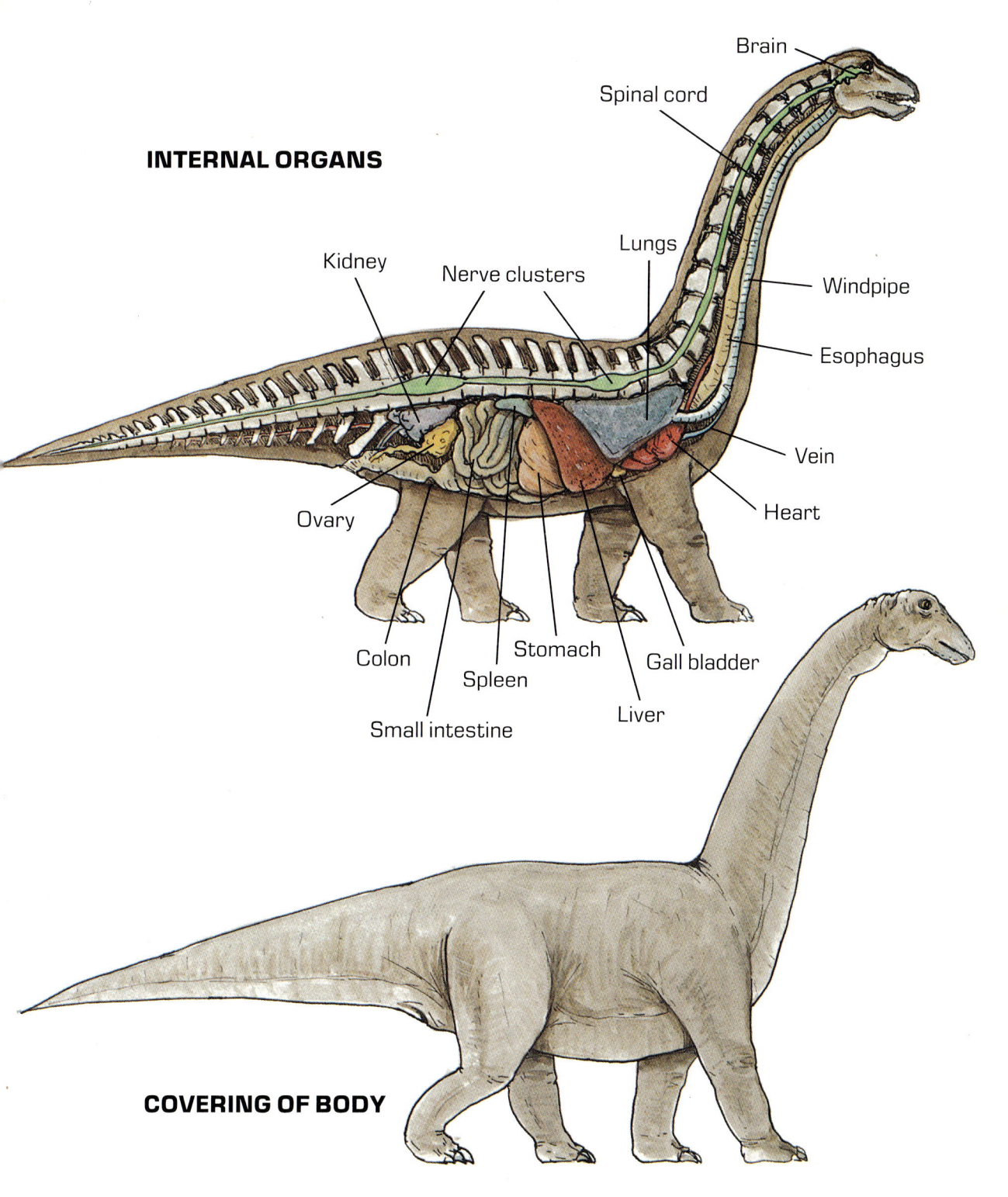

INTERNAL ORGANS

- Brain
- Spinal cord
- Kidney
- Nerve clusters
- Lungs
- Windpipe
- Esophagus
- Vein
- Heart
- Ovary
- Colon
- Spleen
- Small intestine
- Stomach
- Gall bladder
- Liver

COVERING OF BODY

15

The tooth of a plant-eating dinosaur (left) looks very different from the tooth of a dinosaur that ate meat (right).

We might learn something about a dinosaur's diet from pieces of fossilized dung, which scientists call coprolites.

The More Clues, the Better

When we are trying to understand what dinosaurs were like, the more clues we can use, the better. Sometimes the fossil evidence includes more than bones and teeth. Scientists have found fossilized egg shells and footprints that have turned to stone. There are even fossils of dinosaur droppings.

By putting together these kinds of clues, we can come up with some useful deductions. For example, the shape of a dinosaur's teeth might tell us whether the animal ate plants or meat. Footprints could indicate the dinosaur's size and whether it walked on two feet or four.

Other kinds of clues come from the environment in which a dinosaur lived. Are the fossil remains found in an area that was dry or swampy? What plants grew there? This kind of information can often be obtained by examining the rock that surrounds the dinosaur fossils and the remains of fossilized plants.

If we can find out about a dinosaur's environment, we can look at modern animals that live in similar surroundings. Perhaps their characteristics and habits can help us to understand how dinosaurs lived.

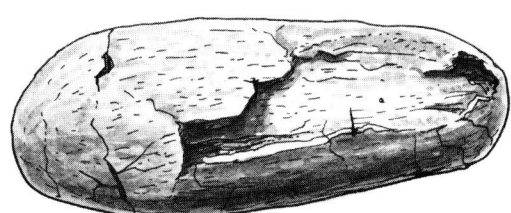

Left: *Under special conditions, pieces of dinosaur skin have been preserved as fossils. This skin is from the crested dinosaur Corythosaurus.* Right: *Fossilized eggs, like this Protoceratops egg, provide valuable information about dinosaur reproduction.*

Above: *These bird-like footprints were left by a dinosaur that probably walked on two legs.* Right: *A large, heavy dinosaur made this deep footprint.*

Dinosaurs with Stripes and Spots?

When we make guesses about the colors and patterns of a dinosaur's skin, we might get some ideas by looking at modern animals.

Dinosaurs are usually considered reptiles. This dinosaur is shown with the same markings as a modern reptile, the python.

Many dinosaurs seem to have lived in tropical climates. Perhaps a white skin like that of the white rhinoceros would have been useful in reflecting the heat of the sun.

Like the giraffe and the zebra, some dinosaurs were probably plant-eaters that roamed over vast plains. Would stripes and spots have made it harder for predators to see the animals in these open areas?

The elephant is the only modern land animal that comes close to the large dinosaurs in size. Here is a dinosaur pictured with the tough, grey skin of this modern giant.

Dinosaurs through the Ages

One of the things that make studying dinosaurs so complicated is the enormous amount of time that the animals lived on earth. Did you know that dinosaurs were on the scene for at least 160 million years? Compared to that incredible span of time, humans have existed for a mere 2 million years.

During their millions of years on this planet, dinosaurs went through many changes. The first dinosaurs, which appeared about

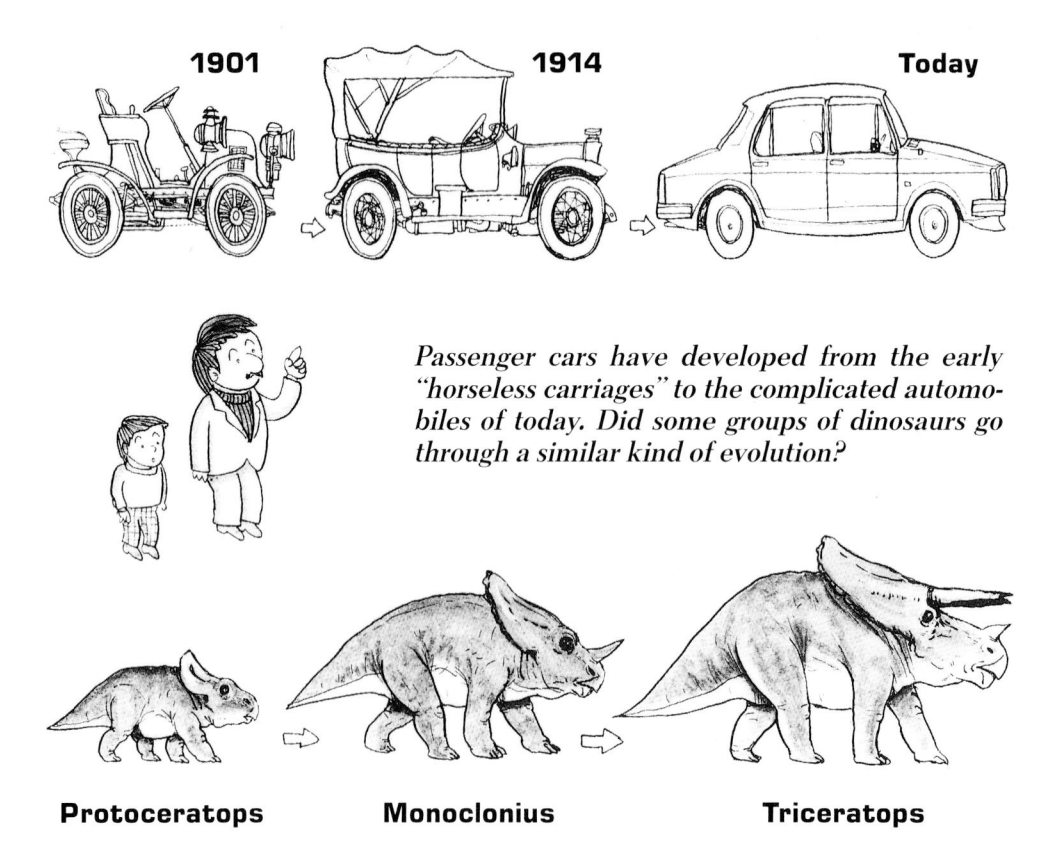

1901 **1914** **Today**

Passenger cars have developed from the early "horseless carriages" to the complicated automobiles of today. Did some groups of dinosaurs go through a similar kind of evolution?

Protoceratops **Monoclonius** **Triceratops**

225 million years ago, gradually developed into a large group of animals with many different characteristics. As the conditions under which they lived changed, dinosaurs also changed so that they could fit into new environments.

Like other living things, dinosaurs evolved through the process of *natural selection.* In a changing environment, a few dinosaurs turned out to have just the physical characteristics that made them successful under the new conditions. Perhaps they happened to have longer necks than other dinosaurs during a period when trees were getting taller. These long-necked dinosaurs would get more food and live to produce offspring that also had long necks. Eventually, the long necks would become the most common kinds of dinosaurs in the land of tall trees. If the environment changed so that tall trees were replaced by low shrubs, then dinosaurs with shorter necks would have an advantage and would gradually become more common.

This is a very simple version of the process that produced the many kinds of dinosaurs. On the next page, you can see another treatment of dinosaur development. Here the artist has used a "family tree" to illustrate the way in which early dinosaurs gradually developed into groups of animals with many different characteristics. The drawing also shows two basic kinds of dinosaurs: the *ornithischians,* which had a hip structure like birds (top part of chart), and the *saurischians,* with hips like lizards (bottom of chart).

For comparison, the artist has also illustrated the evolution of motor vehicles, beginning with the first automobile, invented in the late 1800s. Of course, the development of a human invention like the automobile is not the same as the natural evolution of dinosaurs. You might find it interesting, however, to compare the ways in which many different forms can come from a simple beginning.

THE EVOLUTION OF DINOSAURS

Protoceratops

Triceratops

Stegoceras

Ornithischians
Dinosaurs with hips like birds

Iguanodon

Parasaurolophus

Ankylosaurus

Ancestor of dinosaurs

Stegosaurus

Plateosaurus

Apatosaurus

Brachiosaurus

Saurischians
Dinosaurs with hips like lizards

Ornitholestes

Allosaurus

Tyrannosaurus

THE DEVELOPMENT OF MOTOR VEHICLES

Vehicles that run on wheels

The first automobile

Vehicles that run on treads or belts

Cranes

Fire engines

Trucks

Three-wheeled trucks

Passenger cars

Bulldozers

Missile tanks

Tanks

The beginning of the Mesozoic era, about 225 million years ago

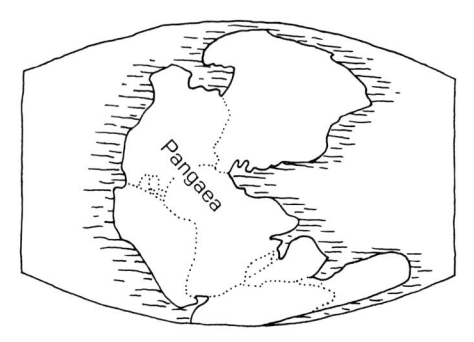

The Age of Dinosaurs

What was the earth like when dinosaurs were alive? There is no simple answer to this question because, as we have seen, dinosaurs were around a very long time.

One of the most important things that happened during the 160 million years of dinosaur existence was a gradual change in the position of the earth's continents. At the beginning of the *Mesozoic era,* when dinosaurs first appeared, all the land on earth was joined in one supercontinent. Scientists call this giant land mass Pangaea, which means "all earth."

During the first period of the Mesozoic era, known as the *Triassic,* Pangaea was inhabited by large numbers of animals, but many familiar modern species were missing. There were insects but no birds, amphibians but no large mammals like elephants, horses, or bears. What the Triassic world had plenty of were reptiles—reptiles that lived in the water and on land, that ran on two feet or walked on four feet. Among them were the early dinosaurs.

The Triassic period lasted 45 million years. Near the end of this time, Pangaea began to break up into the continents of today. During the next period of the Mesozoic era, the *Jurassic,* the continents slowly drifted apart, carrying with them members of

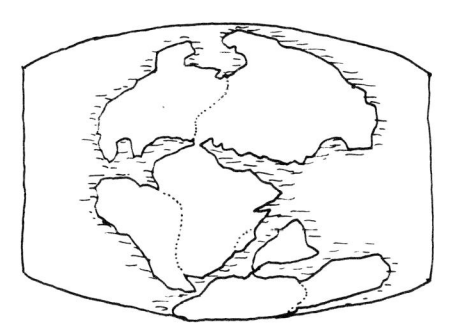

The end of the Triassic period, about 180 million years ago

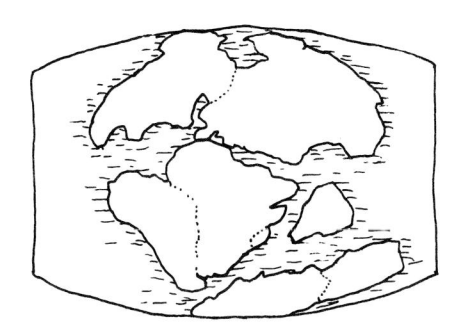

The end of the Jurassic period, about 135 million years ago

the rapidly developing tribe of dinosaurs. The Jurassic was a true age of dinosaurs, with many different kinds occupying the most important positions in the animal world. During this period, the ancestors of modern birds appeared on the scene. Small mammals were present, but they were overshadowed by the ruling reptiles.

The *Cretaceous,* the last period of the Mesozoic era, began about 135 million years ago. During most of this period, dinosaurs continued to dominate the world, but changes were beginning to take place. New dinosaur groups appeared, some of them very strange in appearance. Birds and flying reptiles filled the sky, and flowering plants grew on land. The continents continued to drift apart, separating animals that had once lived together.

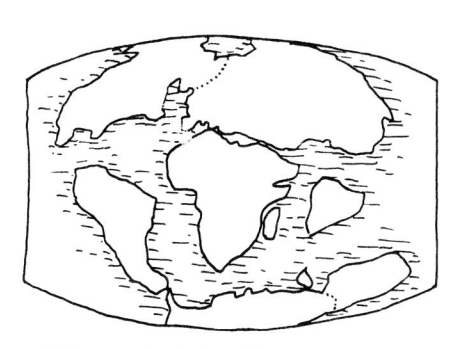

The end of the Cretaceous period, about 65 million years ago

Near the end of the Cretaceous period, about 65 million years ago, life on earth was drastically changed by some catastrophe. Many kinds of animals ceased to exist, including dinosaurs. Mammals survived and came out of their hiding places, ready to play a larger role in the life of the planet.

THE MESOZOIC ERA

TRIASSIC PERIOD   225 to 180 million years ago

Plateosaurus

JURASSIC PERIOD   180 to 135 million years ago

Rhamphorhynchus

Stegosaurus

CRETACEOUS PERIOD   135 to 65 million years ago

Quetzalcoatlus

Anatosaurus

Ankylosaurus

Tyrannosaurus

Coelophysis
Lystrosaurus
Triassochelys

Apatosaurus
Allosaurus
Archaeopteryx

Triceratops

The Case of Stegosaurus

Now that we have some information about dinosaurs in general, let's take a look at some particular dinosaurs. Our first subject is Stegosaurus.

This dinosaur lived about 150 million years ago, during the Jurassic period. Remains of Stegosaurus have been found in North America, and similar dinosaurs have turned up in Africa and Asia. All the members of the stegosaur group had front legs that were shorter than their hind legs. They seem to have walked on all four legs. Based on the evidence of their blunt teeth, they were probably plant eaters.

The most unusual physical feature of Stegosaurus was a set of large, flat pieces of bone located on the dinosaur's back. These bone plates have been found in many excavations of Stegosaurus fossils. But exactly how were they arranged, and what purpose did they serve?

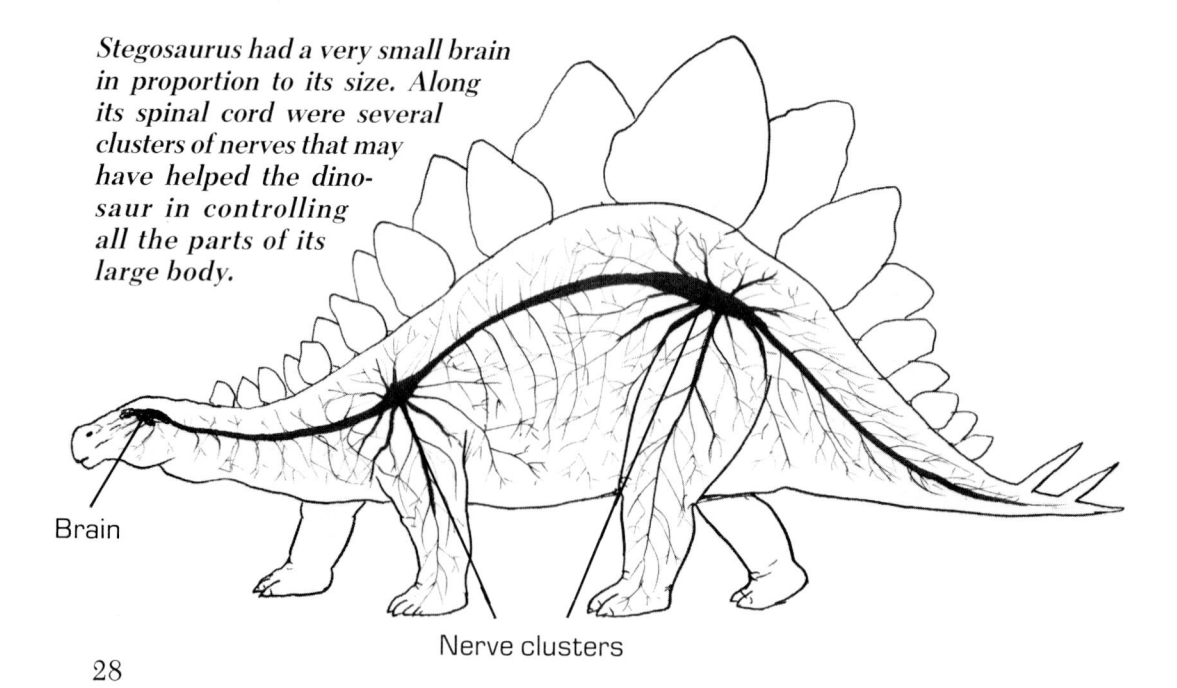

Stegosaurus had a very small brain in proportion to its size. Along its spinal cord were several clusters of nerves that may have helped the dinosaur in controlling all the parts of its large body.

Brain

Nerve clusters

Stegosaurus's most unusual features were the flat bone plates on its back.

Stegosaurus was similar in size to the African elephant.

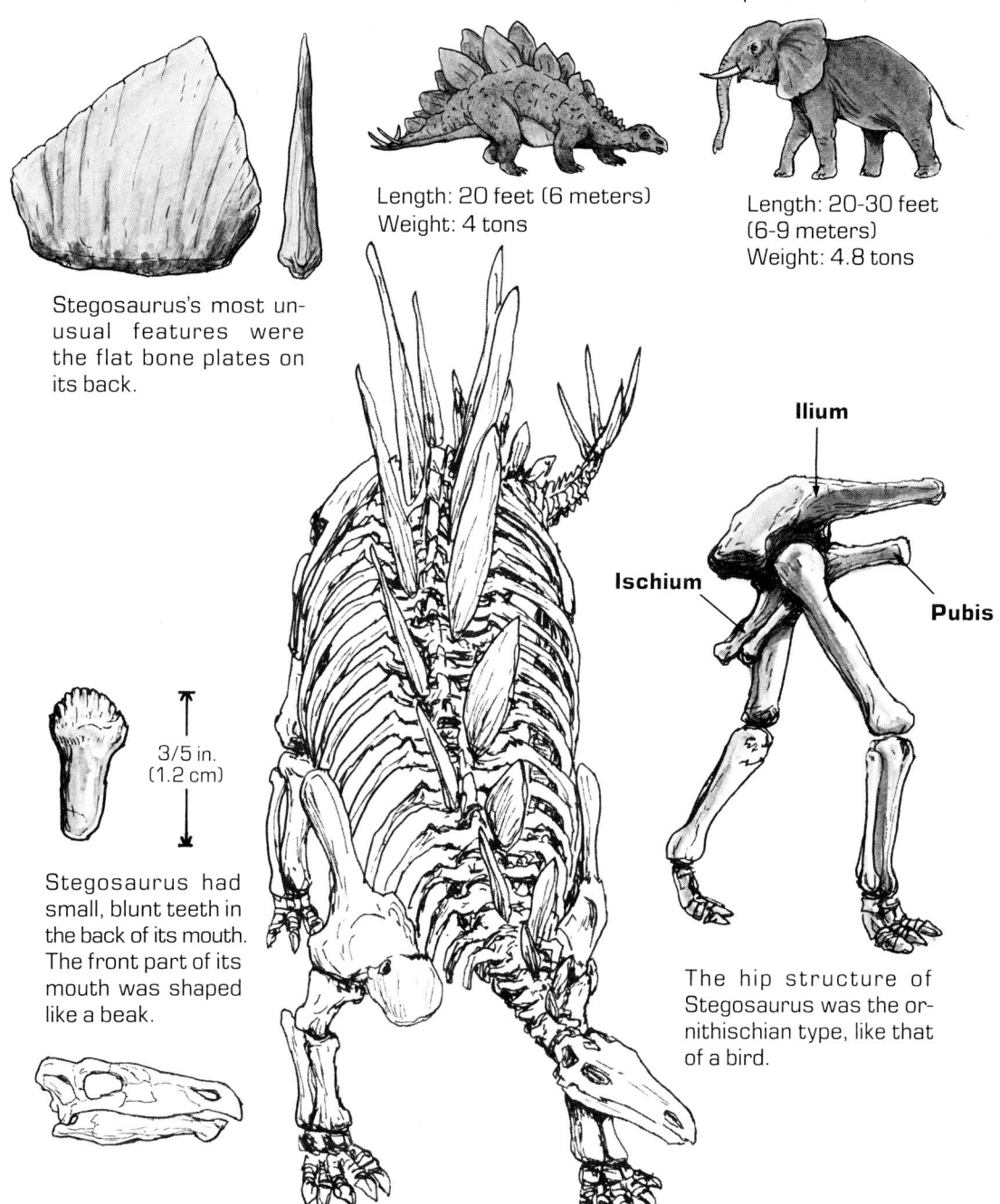

Length: 20 feet (6 meters)
Weight: 4 tons

Length: 20-30 feet (6-9 meters)
Weight: 4.8 tons

Ilium

Ischium

Pubis

3/5 in. (1.2 cm)

Stegosaurus had small, blunt teeth in the back of its mouth. The front part of its mouth was shaped like a beak.

The hip structure of Stegosaurus was the ornithischian type, like that of a bird.

RECONSTRUCTION OF A STEGOSAURUS SKELETON

Many scientists used to think that Stegosaurus's plates were arranged in a vertical position in two rows on the dinosaur's back. The plates on the right and left sides alternated with each other in a kind of zig-zag pattern (below).

Stegosaurus with plates standing up

Stegosaurus with plates hanging down over its sides

Now some people think that the plates might have been arranged in pairs and that they might have been held in a horizontal instead of a vertical position (above). In this way, they would have protected the sides of Stegosaurus's body.

31

In many excavations of Stegosaurus fossils, the plates were found scattered, leaving scientists with a puzzle to solve.

What to Do with Stegosaurus's Plates?

Everyone agrees that Stegosaurus's plates belong on its back, but there are a lot of different theories about how the plates were positioned.

One of the earliest ideas about the plates was that they were arranged not in pairs but alternating with each other. Many scientists accepted this theory because fossilized plates had been found buried in this position in an early excavation. The fact that no two plates were exactly the same size also made paleontologists think that they did not come in pairs.

But now some scientists believe that this evidence is not strong enough to make a case about the position of Stegosaurus's plates.

They point out that the alternating arrangement of the plates in an excavation could have been an accident. It might have been caused by shifts in position that took place after the dinosaur died.

Another fact to consider is that this kind of uneven arrangement of parts on two sides of the body is very rare among present-day animals with backbones. There is also the evidence of several other members of the stegosaur group that seem to have had paired plates on their backs. Why would Stegosaurus be so different from its relatives and from modern animals?

The argument about how Stegosaurus's plates were arranged has still not been settled. Today there are some scientists who have another idea about this unsolved problem. They think that the plates might have been arranged in a single row down the middle of the dinosaur's back rather than in two rows.

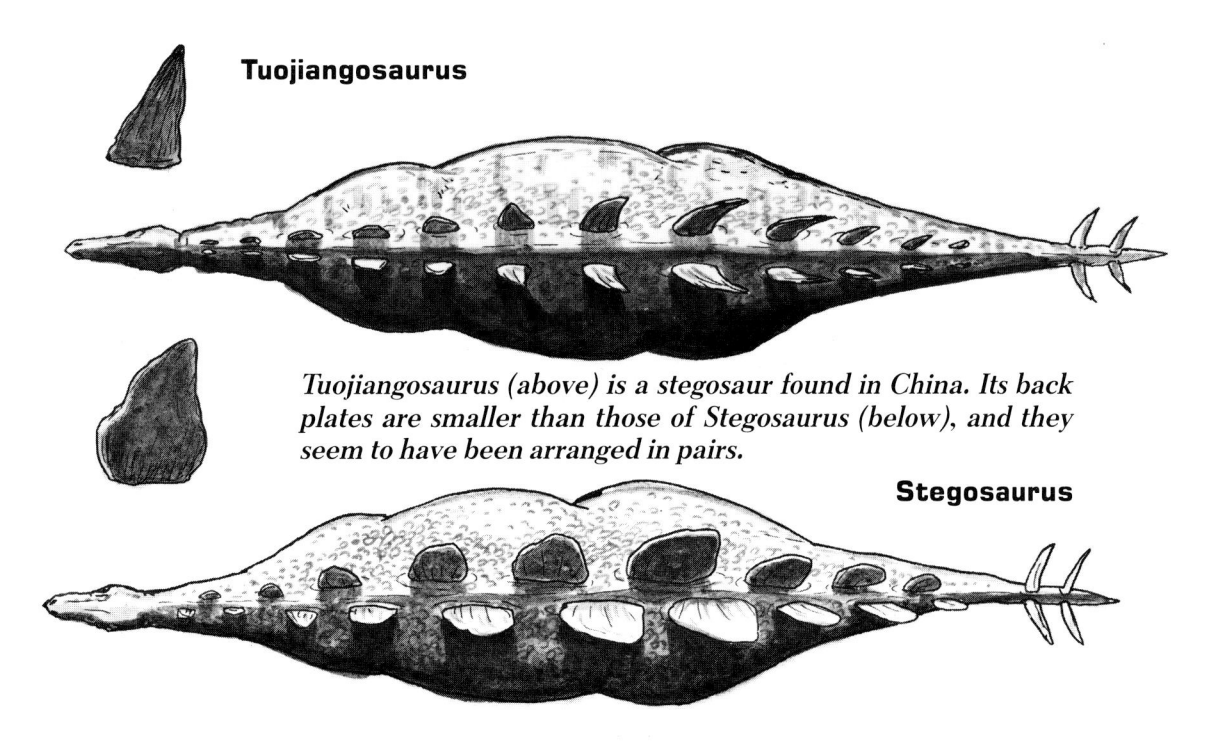

Tuojiangosaurus

Tuojiangosaurus (above) is a stegosaur found in China. Its back plates are smaller than those of Stegosaurus (below), and they seem to have been arranged in pairs.

Stegosaurus

Plates and Spikes for Self-Defense?

What was the purpose of Stegosaurus's plates? Many scientists believe that they were used for self-defense. In addition to plates, stegosaurs and their relatives, the ankylosaurs, were equipped with spikes and other body parts that could have served as armor or as weapons.

Kentrosaurus

A stegosaur living in Africa during the Jurassic period, Kentrosaurus had pairs of plates on its back and spikes extending from its two hips.

Tuojiangosaurus

Tuojiangosaurus was a Jurassic stegosaur from China with paired plates on its back and four spikes on its tail.

Polacanthus

An early ankylosaur, or armored dinosaur, from the Cretaceous period, Polacanthus had spikes lined up along its back and bone plates on its tail.

This scene shows the way in which Stegosaurus might have used its plates to protect its body against the attack of a fierce, meat-eating Allosaurus.

Defense against Attack

If Stegosaurus's plates were meant for self-defense, there are several ways in which they could have been put to use. In addition to shielding the dinosaur's body from attack (as shown on the previous page), they might have served to frighten predators away. Some paleontologists think that the pairs of plates usually hung down over Stegosaurus's side. When the dinosaur was threatened by an enemy, the plates were brought suddenly into a vertical position. This would have made Stegosaurus look larger and more dangerous. Perhaps the plates were even clapped together to make a loud, frightening noise.

We know that some modern animals, including reptiles, defend themselves by making noises and expanding their bodies. Maybe Stegosaurus used the same methods millions of years ago.

Stegosaurus's plates might have been used as a kind of camouflage so that the dinosaur could hide from predators (above). If the camouflage failed, Stegosaurus could have fought off a predator with the long spikes on its tail (below).

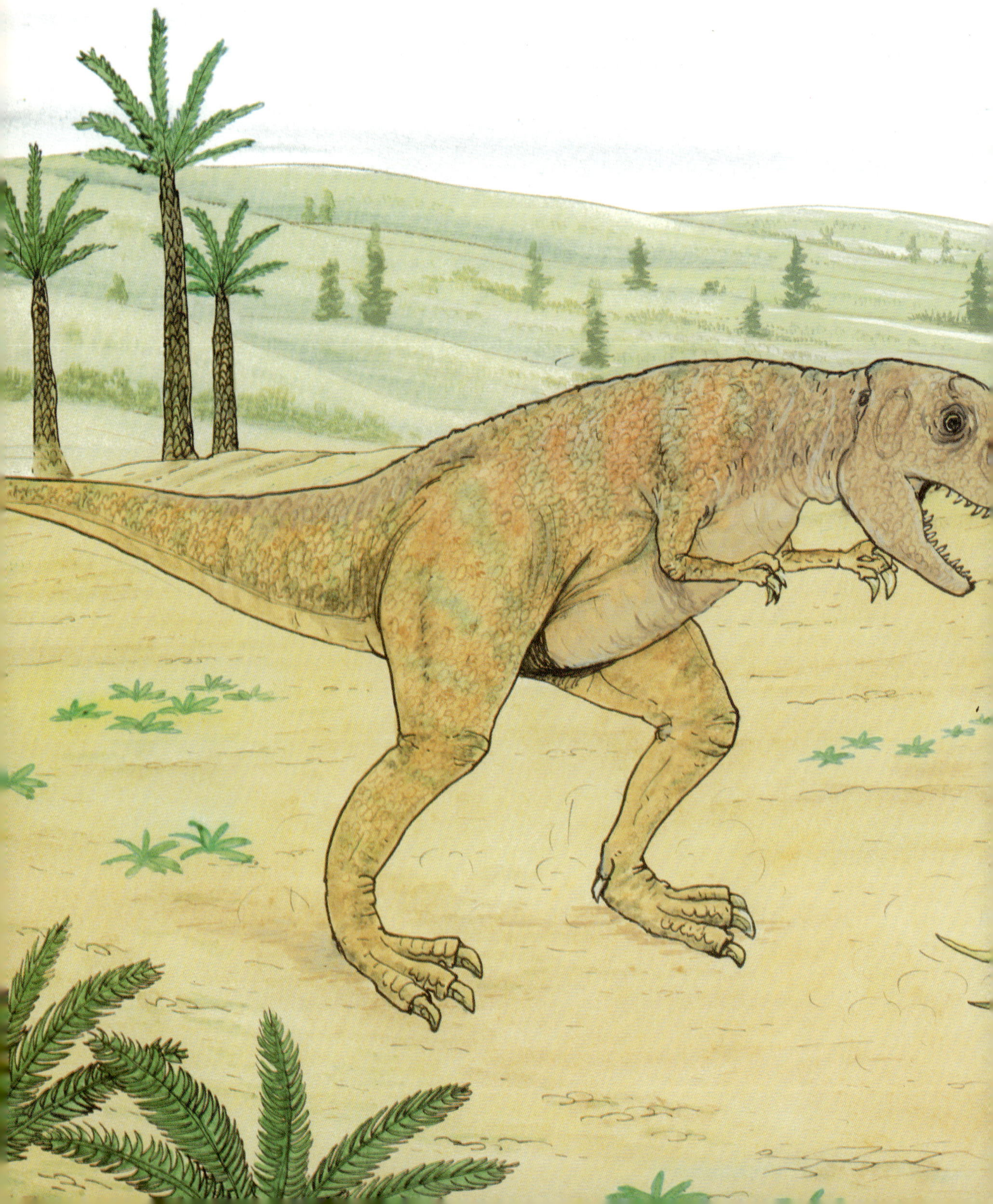

Here is another way that Stegosaurus might have protected itself from attack. By lying on the ground and curling up, the dinosaur could turn itself into a large ball with hard plates sticking out all around.

Other Ideas about Stegosaurus's Plates

Some scientists don't believe that self-defense was the main purpose of Stegosaurus's plates. They have other ideas about these strange features.

One idea is that the plates helped to regulate Stegosaurus's temperature. If dinosaurs were reptiles, as many people believe, then they probably had no inner control over their body temperatures. Like modern reptiles, they were *ectotherms,* animals whose temperatures are controlled by the temperature of their surroundings. (Another word for this condition is "cold-blooded.")

Stegosaurus's plates might have helped in temperature control by acting as a kind of radiator. Grooves in the plates suggest that they may have had a lot of large blood vessels running through

Stegosaurus's plates may have absorbed heat when turned toward the sun. This could have helped to raise the dinosaur's body temperature in cool weather.

When Stegosaurus was too hot, the many blood vessels on the surface of its plates could have helped to release heat and lower the dinosaur's temperature.

them. These blood vessels could have absorbed heat from the sun when the dinosaur was cold. When Stegosaurus was too hot, heat could have been released from its body through the blood vessels in its plates.

The radiator theory about Stegosaurus's plates is based on the belief that dinosaurs were ectotherms, like modern reptiles. Today an increasing number of scientists believe that at least some dinosaurs may have been *endotherms*, animals with body temperatures that were internally controlled. There is a lot of disagreement among experts on this question, and Stegosaurus's plates are part of the controversy.

Another, very different, idea about Stegosaurus's plates is that they may have helped the dinosaur to find a mate. Perhaps only male stegosaurs had plates, and they used them to attract females, in the same way that male birds use brightly colored feathers. This is another interesting theory about Stegosaurus that can never really be proved.

The Case of Apatosaurus

Here is another dinosaur that has been the subject of much investigation. Apatosaurus belongs to the group of large plant-eating dinosaurs known as *sauropods*. It lived during the late Jurassic period in North America and Europe and was a true giant, 60 to 85 feet (18 to 25 meters) long and with an estimated weight of 30 tons.

This dinosaur is often known as Brontosaurus, but its correct scientific name is Apatosaurus. This name was the first given to it when fossils of the dinosaur were discovered.

Sauropods around the World

Brachiosaurus
Length: 100 feet (30 meters)
Weight: 70 tons
Late Jurassic-early Cretaceous
North America, Europe, Africa

Diplodocus
Length: 90 feet (27 meters)
Weight: 10 tons
Late Jurassic, North America

Mamenchisaurus
Length: 74 feet (22 meters)
Weight: 30 tons
Late Jurassic, China

Camarasaurus
Length: 60 feet (18 meters)
Weight: 25 tons
Late Jurassic-early Cretaceous
North America, Europe

How Did Apatosaurus Live?

The case of Apatosaurus involves a different kind of puzzle than the mystery of Stegosaurus's plates. Fossil remains of Apatosaurus and many other sauropods have been found, and there are no unusual body parts to account for. We have a good idea of how these giant animals were constructed. (Some of the facts about Apatosaurus are shown on these two pages.)

Instead, the mystery concerns the dinosaurs' way of life. What kind of environment did Apatosaurus and other sauropods live in? What did they eat and how did they eat it? These are some of the basic questions that people are asking about Apatosaurus and its relatives.

THE WRONG SKULL

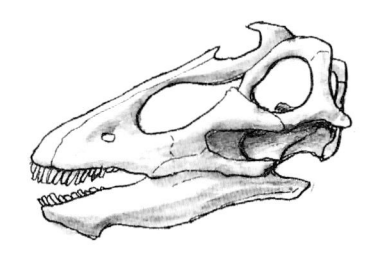

For many years, most reconstructions of Apatosaurus showed the dinosaur with a broad, short skull and fairly strong teeth (above left). Skulls like this had been found in early excavations near other Apatosaurus bones, and scientists thought that they belonged to the big dinosaurs. Later excavations, however, unearthed a different skull, this one long and narrow, with small, weak teeth (above right). Today most scientists think that this second skull is the correct one, even though no Apatosaurus skeleton has ever been found with a skull still attached. The first skull probably belonged to another sauropod, Camarasaurus.

Apatosaurus and other sauropods belong to the saurischian group of dinosaurs because their hips are like those of lizards.

Ilium

Ischium

Pubis

Light neck bones

Small head

Thick leg bones

The skeleton of Apatosaurus is strong but light.

Eye socket

Nasal socket

Eye socket

Nasal socket

Many sauropods have nostrils or nasal sockets on the tops of their heads.

BRACHIOSAURUS

CAMARASAURUS

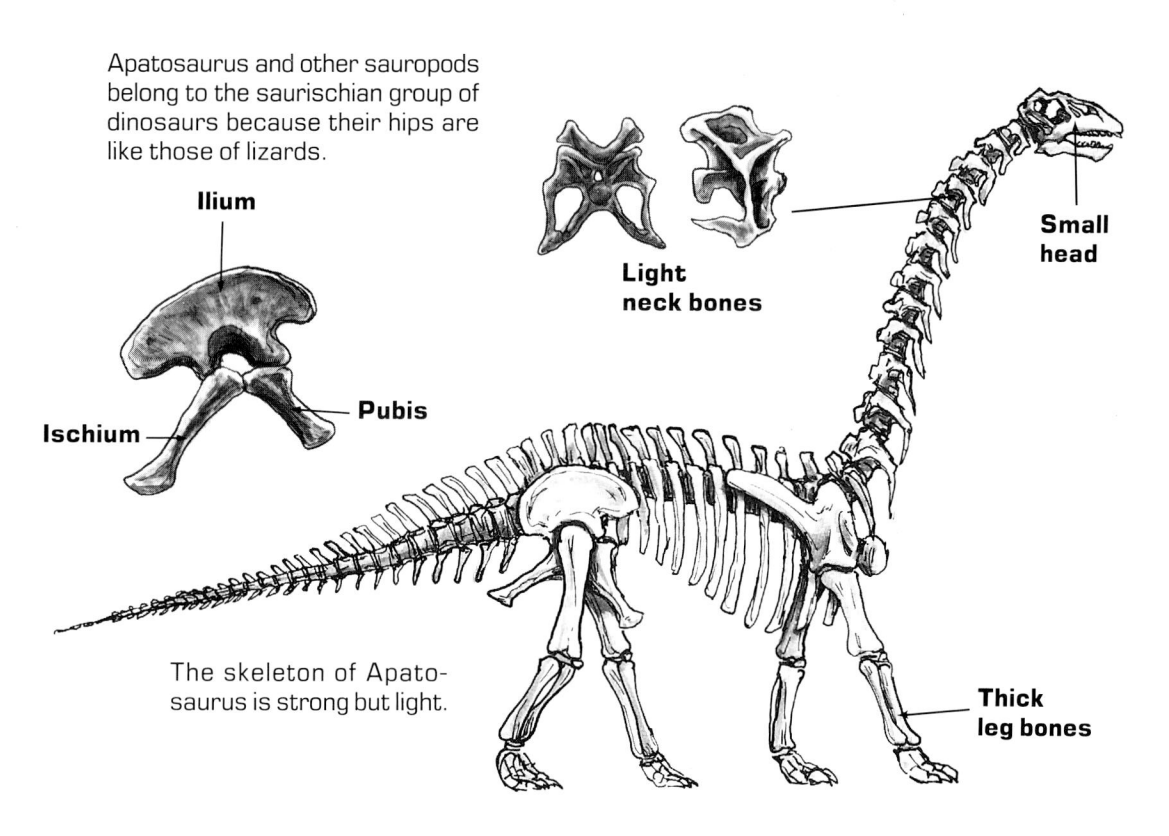

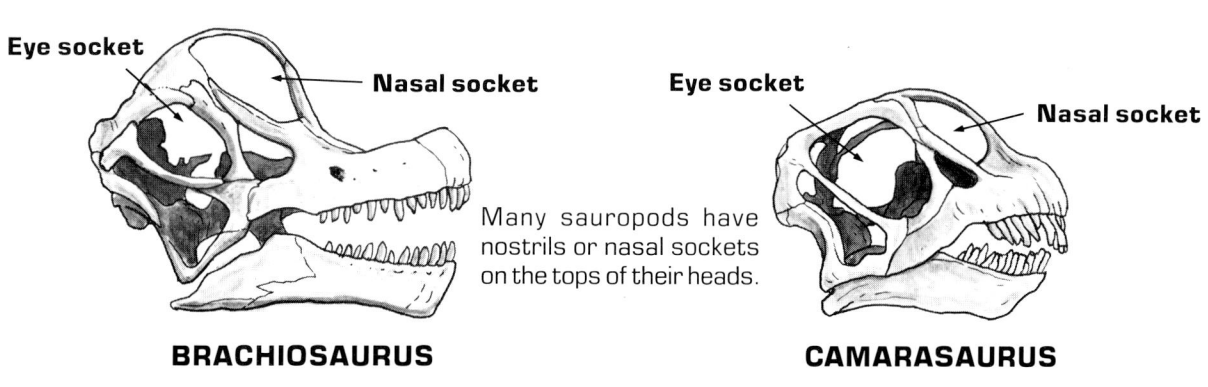

Sauropods had long, heavy tails, but the prints they left usually show no marks of tails being dragged on the ground.

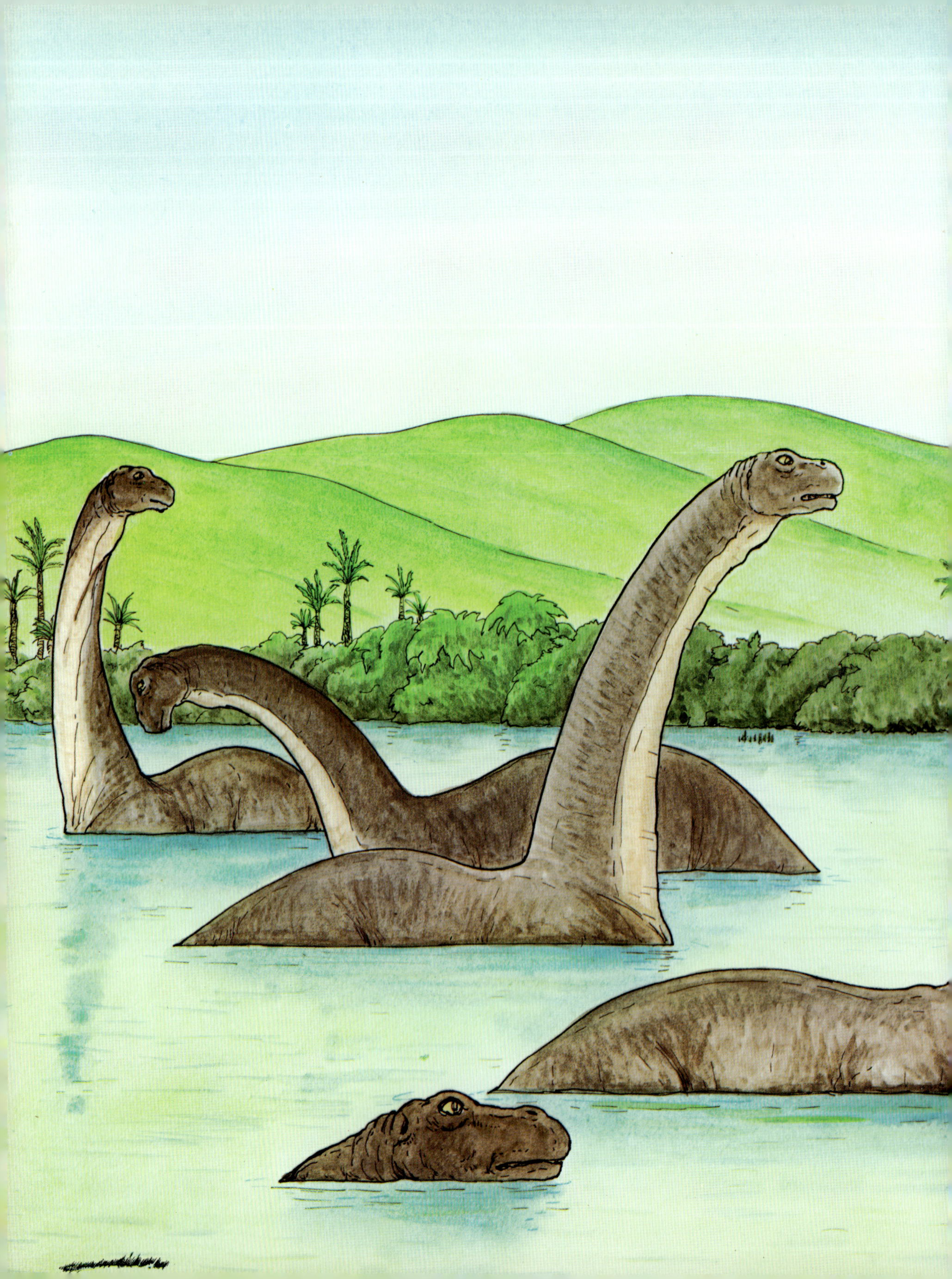

When sauropod fossils were first discovered, people thought that the huge animals were something like whales and that they lived in the ocean. Even after scientists realized that Apatosaurus and other sauropods were not related to whales, many still believed that the dinosaurs spent most of their time in lakes and marshes.

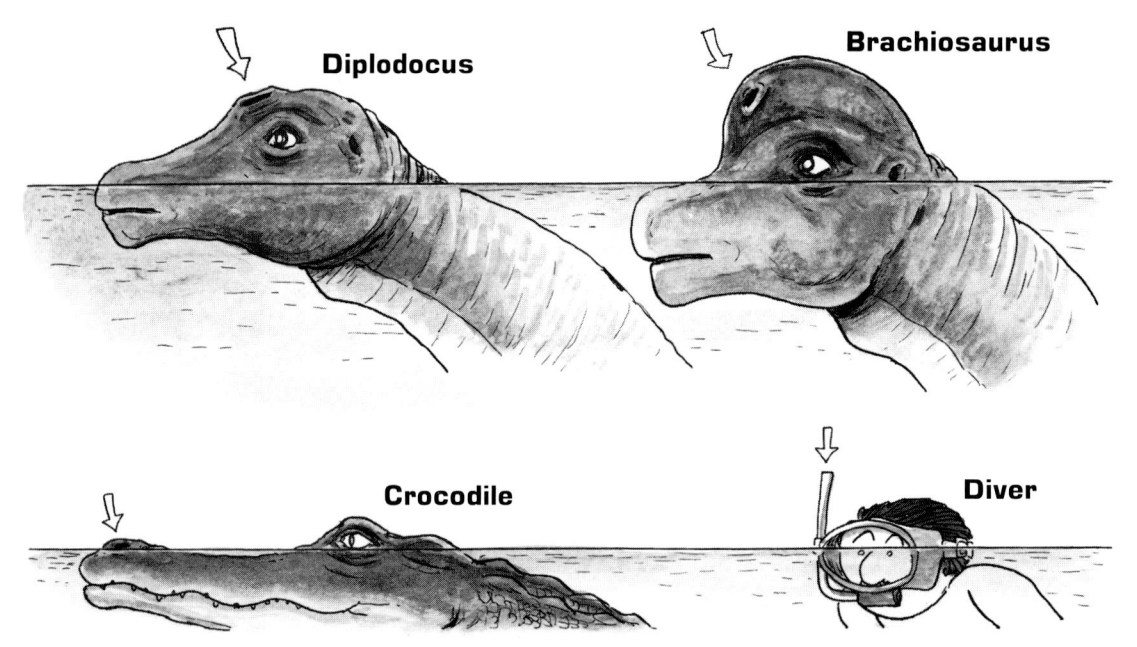

These sauropods are shown breathing through their nostrils with their bodies underwater. Crocodiles use this method of breathing, while human divers have snorkels that extend above the water's surface.

A Life in Water?

What are the reasons for thinking that Apatosaurus was a water animal? Here are some of the most important ones.

First is the enormous size of Apatosaurus and many other sauropods. These dinosaurs were much bigger than modern land animals like elephants. How could Apatosaurus or Brachiosaurus have walked around carrying such great weight? Wouldn't it have been much easier for them to live in lakes, where the water would support their giant bodies?

If Apatosaurus lived in water, then it might have eaten the soft plants that often grow around lakes and marshes. These eating habits would help to explain why this dinosaur and some other sauropods had such small, weak teeth. A life in water would also explain another characteristic of many sauropods—the location of their nostrils on the tops of their heads. This useful arrangement may have allowed the dinosaurs to breathe with most of their bodies underwater, using their long necks as a kind of snorkel.

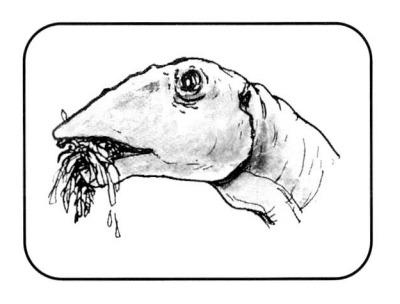

Is there any fossil evidence to suggest that Apatosaurus and other sauropods lived in water? Some fossil footprints found in Texas seem to support this idea. The prints were light impressions made by the front feet of several sauropods. Scientists believe that they were left by dinosaurs that were floating in a lake and using their front feet to push themselves gently along (below). These sauropods at least spent some of their time in deep water.

When sauropods walked on the bottoms of lakes, did their heavy legs hold them down in the same way as the heavy boots worn by this diver? This is one of the theories about the dinosaurs' underwater life.

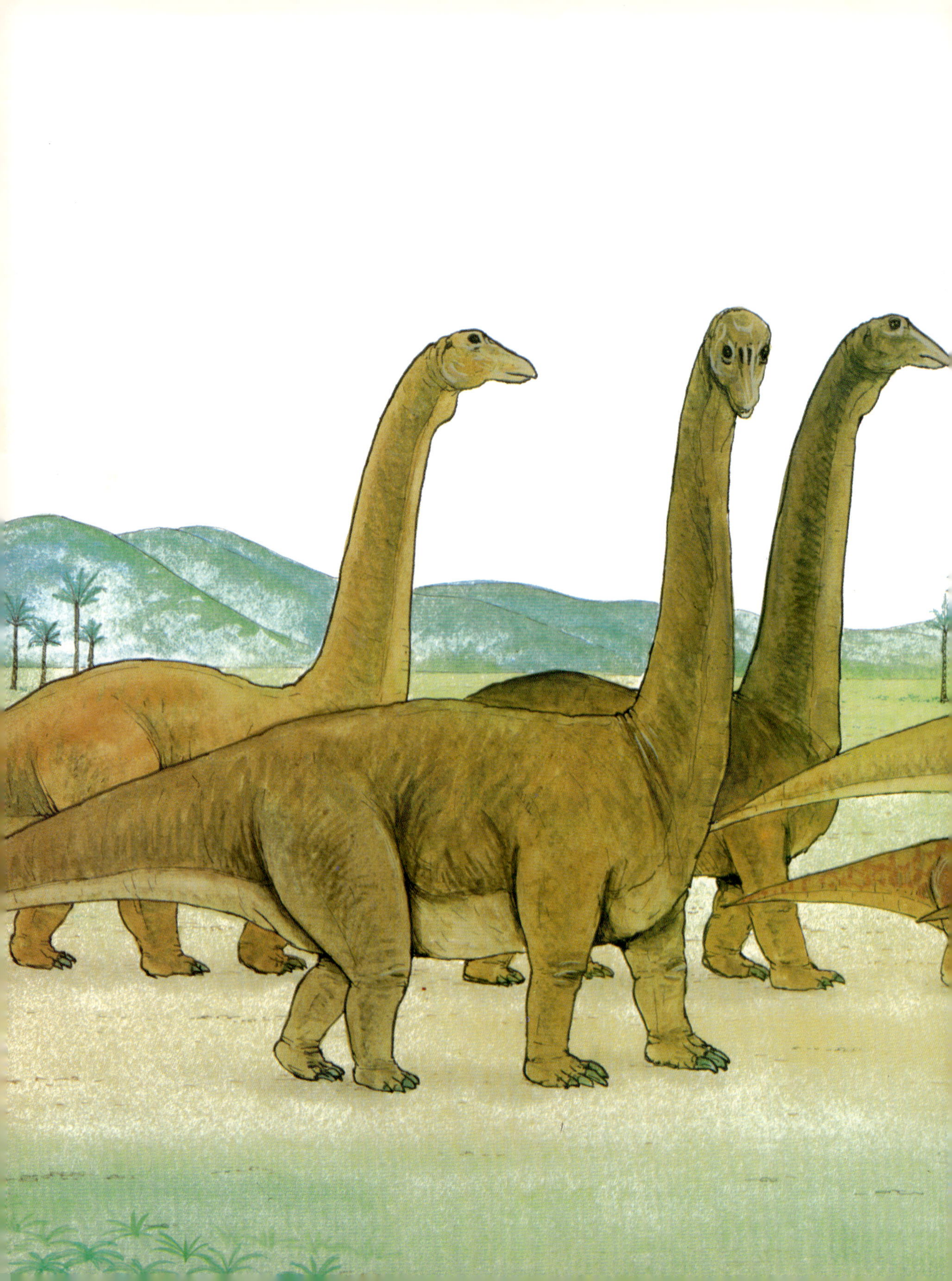

In recent years, many paleontologists have come to believe that sauropods were basically land animals, living a life something like that of a modern elephant. This illustration shows a group of sauropods traveling together, with some young animals in their midst.

Many experts now believe that dinosaurs as large as Brachiosaurus would not have been able to breathe with their bodies submerged in deep water.

A Life on Land?

Why have some scientists changed their minds about Apatosaurus's way of living? They have come to different conclusions simply by looking at the same evidence from another point of view.

The great size of Apatosaurus and other sauropods was once seen as evidence of their living in water. Now most experts say that such large, long-necked animals could not possibly have breathed with their bodies completely submerged in water. If Diplodocus or Brachiosaurus stood on the bottom of a lake with only their heads sticking out, their lungs would have been at least 30 feet (9 meters) below the water's surface. At this depth, the water pressure on their bodies would have made it very difficult for the animals to inflate their lungs. These facts have convinced most people that although sauropods may have waded in shallow lakes or marshes, they did not spend a lot of time in deep water.

A closer look at the skeletons of these big dinosaurs has also given support to the idea that they lived on land rather than in water. The bones of their necks and backs are usually strong but light, some having large open spaces in them. The leg bones, on the other hand, are very thick and heavy. With this kind of construction, sauropods would probably have been able to move their heavy bodies around on land more easily than scientists had earlier thought.

Below: *Because of its light, strong skeleton, Apatosaurus may have been able to hold its head and tail up instead of letting them hang down as had been earlier thought.*

Left: *Apatosaurus's thick, column-like legs were probably strong enough to support the dinosaur's small head and the light bones in its long neck.*

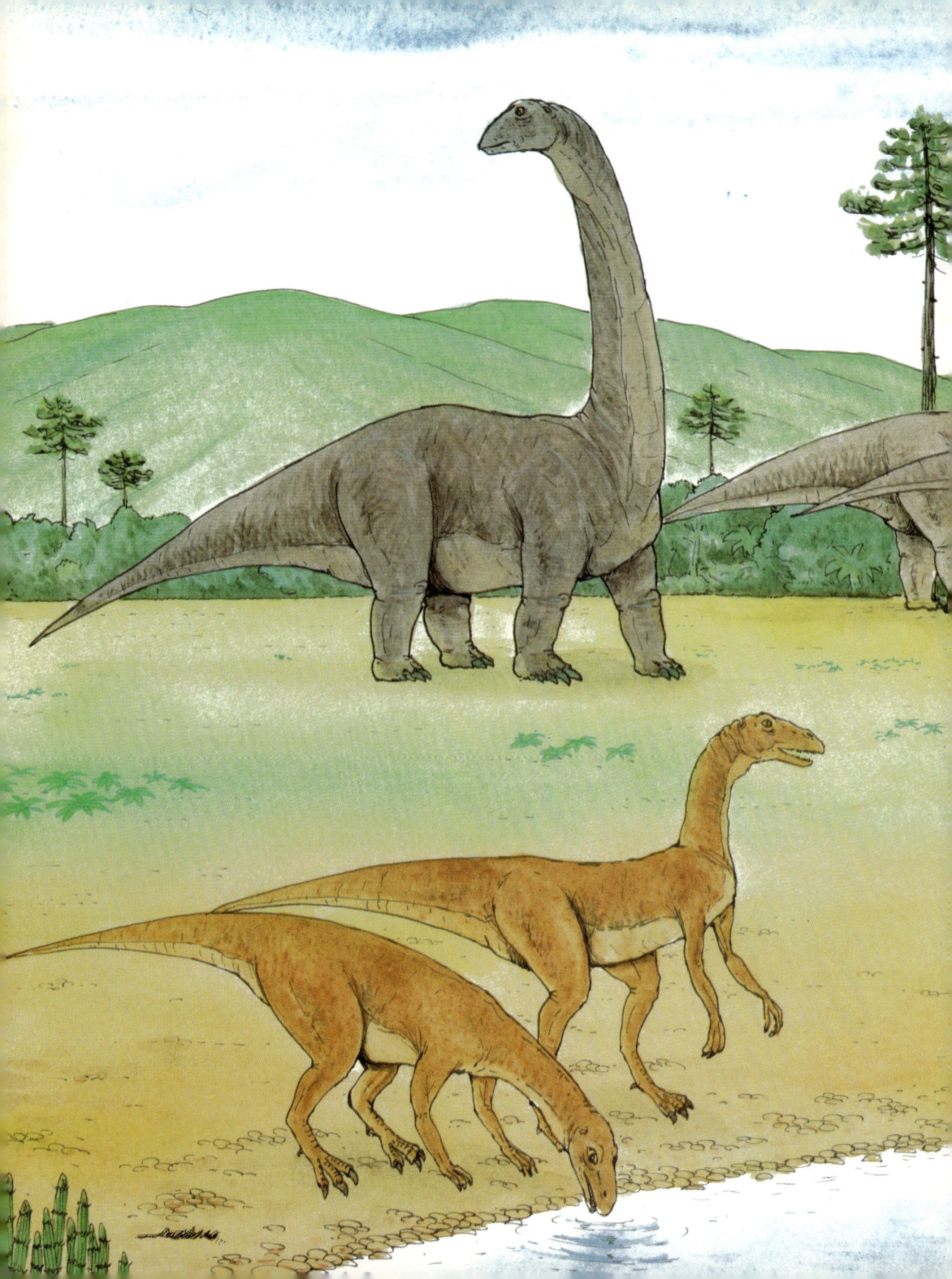

If sauropods were land animals, what kind of lives did they lead? This picture illustrates one of the possible answers to this question. It shows some Apatosauruses feeding together in a herd, as elephants do today. While most of the herd members are eating, one dinosaur keeps watch against predators that might attack the group.

Like elephants, Apatosaurus and other sauropods living in herds might have been related to each other. Older members of the group could have helped to guard and take care of the young dinosaurs.

A Diet of Needles and Twigs?

If sauropods lived on land, they probably didn't eat water plants. Many paleontologists think that they might have fed on the tough needles and leaves of conifer trees. These evergreen trees were common during the Jurassic period, when sauropods were on the scene. The dinosaurs' long necks would have made it easy for them to feed on the tall conifers (right), just as giraffes today eat the leaves of tall trees on the African plains.

The weak teeth of many sauropods would not have been suitable for chewing conifer needles and twigs. But they could have been used to pull needles and twigs off the trees. In fact, some fossil sauropod teeth show the kind of wear that might have resulted from such use.

How did sauropods digest such tough food if they were unable to chew it? Some scientists think that they had *gizzards*, digestive organs possessed by modern birds and crocodiles. A gizzard is a pouch with walls made of thick muscles that contract, grinding the food inside. To aid in this "chewing" process, birds and crocodiles swallow gravel and small stones that act as "teeth" in their gizzards. In some excavations of sauropod fossils, large numbers of smooth, polished stones have been found. Some people believe that these stones came from the dinosaurs' gizzards.

A Glimpse into the Past

Apatosaurus and other sauropods ate plants, but they shared the earth with meat-eating dinosaurs that were always looking for a meal. In a herd, sauropods might have been protected from the attack of predators like Allosaurus (above). But a sauropod alone, especially one that was old or sick, was not so safe.

Some fossil footprints found in Texas seem to tell the story of one sauropod whose life was in danger. The prints suggest that the big dinosaur was being followed by a large meat-eater similar to Allosaurus. In some places, the three-toed predator stepped inside the enormous footprints left by the sauropod. The picture on the next page presents an artist's version of this dramatic scene.

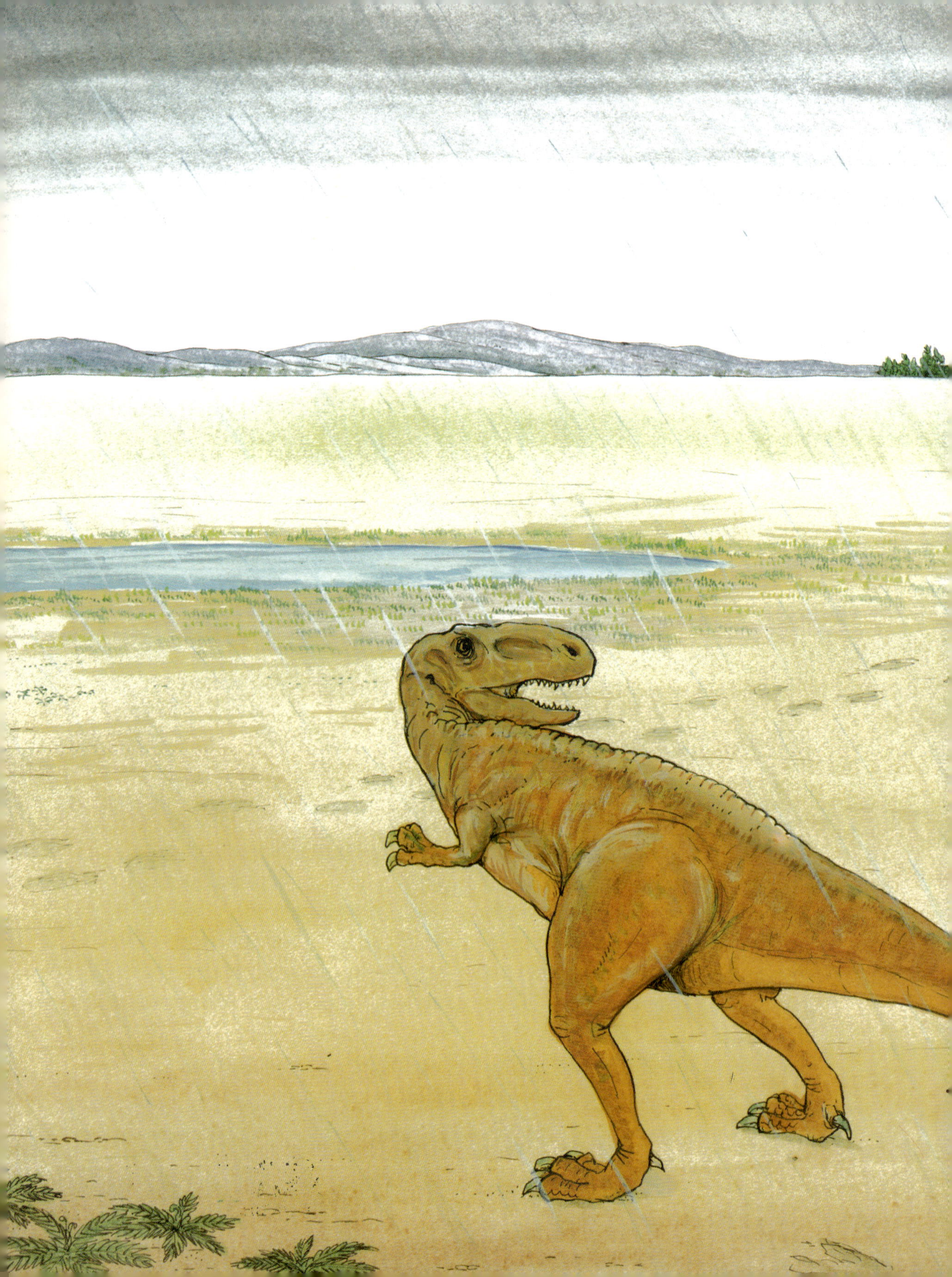

Did the pursuit end in attack or escape? We will never know, for the story told by the fossil footprints is incomplete. Even though we don't know how the story ended, the fossils give us a revealing glimpse into the past and help us to understand how dinosaurs lived.

Dinosaurs Included in This Book

Allosaurus (al-uh-SAW-ruhs)—a meat-eating dinosaur from the Jurassic period in North America

Anatosaurus (uh-nat-uh-SAW-ruhs)—a hadrosaur, or duck-billed dinosaur, from the Cretaceous period in North America

Ankylosaurus (an-kile-uh-SAW-ruhs)—an armored dinosaur from the Cretaceous period in North America

Apatosaurus (uh-pat-uh-SAW-ruhs)—a large plant-eating dinosaur, or sauropod, from the Jurassic period in North America. This dinosaur is often called Brontosaurus.

Archaeopteryx (ar-kee-OP-teh-ricks)—a small dinosaur with feathers or the first bird, depending on your point of view. Fossils of Archeopteryx from the Jurassic period have been found in Germany.

Brachiosaurus (brack-ee-uh-SAW-ruhs)—a very large sauropod from the Jurassic period. Fossils found in North America and Africa.

Camarasaurus (kam-uh-ruh-SAW-ruhs)—a Jurassic sauropod from North America

Coelophysis (see-loh-FI-siss)—a small Triassic dinosaur from North America, one of the earliest theropods, or meat-eaters

Corythosaurus (ko-rith-uh-SAW-ruhs)—a hadrosaur from the Cretaceous period in North America. Like many hadrosaurs, Corythosaurus had a bony crest on its head.

Diplodocus (dih-PLOD-uh-kus)—a Jurassic sauropod from North America

Iguanodon (ih-GWA-nih-don)—a large plant-eating dinosaur from the Cretaceous period in Europe. The fossils of Iguanodon were among the earliest discovered in the 1800s.

Kentrosaurus (ken-tro-SAW-ruhs)—a stegosaur, or plated dinosaur, from the Jurassic period in Africa

Mamenchisaurus (mah-men-kih-SAW-ruhs)—a long-necked sauropod from the Jurassic period in China

Monoclonius (mo-noh-KLO-nee-us)—an early ceratopsian, or horned dinosaur, from the Cretaceous period in North America

Ornitholestes (or-nith-oh-LES-teez)—a small meat-eating dinosaur from the Jurassic period in North America

Parasaurolophus (par-uh-sawr-AWL-uh-fus)—a hadrosaur from the Cretaceous period in North America

Plateosaurus (plat-ee-oh-SAW-ruhs)—a large Triassic dinosaur that was the ancestor of the sauropods. Fossils found in Europe.

Polacanthus (pohl-uh-KAN-thuhs)—an armored dinosaur from the Cretaceous period in England

Protoceratops (pro-toe-SER-uh-tops)—an early ceratopsian from the Cretaceous period in Asia

Stegosaurus (steg-uh-SAW-ruhs)—a large plated dinosaur from the Jurassic period in North America

Triceratops (tri-SER-uh-tops)—a ceratopsian with three horns. From the Cretaceous period in North America.

Tuojiangosaurus (too-jon-go-SAW-ruhs)—a Jurassic stegosaur from China

Tyrannosaurus (tih-ran-uh-SAW-ruhs)—the largest of the meat-eating dinosaurs. From the Cretaceous period in North America.

Glossary

Cretaceous (creh-TAY-shus) period—the third and last part of the Mesozoic era

ectotherms (EK-toh-therms)—animals whose body temperatures are controlled by the temperature of the environment. Modern reptiles and insects are ectotherms.

endotherms (EN-doh-therms)—animals whose body temperatures are controlled from within. Birds and mammals are endotherms.

fossils—remains or traces of animals and plants that lived in the past. Sometimes bones, teeth, or shells are fossilized and preserved by minerals that fill small air spaces within them. Other kinds of fossils are footprints or impressions made in mud that later turns to rock.

gizzards—digestive organs with thick, muscular walls that contract to grind food. Some scientists think that dinosaurs, like modern birds and crocodiles, had gizzards and that they swallowed stones to aid in the grinding process.

Jurassic (juh-RASS-ik) period—the middle part of the Mesozoic era

Mesozoic (mehz-oh-ZOH-ik) era—the 160-million-year period of earth history during which dinosaurs lived. The Mesozoic era is divided into three parts: the Triassic, the Jurassic, and the Cretaceous periods.

natural selection—the process by which animals or plants with characteristics best suited to their environment tend to survive and to produce offspring with the same characteristics. By means of natural selection, a group of organisms may gradually change in response to changes in the environment.

ornithischians (awr-nih-THIS-kee-uhns)—dinosaurs with hips similiar to those of birds. The dinosaurs in this group were all plant eaters.

paleontologists (pay-lee-ohn-TAHL-uh-jists)—scientists who study prehistoric life

saurischians (saw-RIS-kee-uhns)—dinosaurs with hips similar to those of lizards. This group includes all the meat-eating dinosaurs and the large plant-eaters known as sauropods.

sauropods (SAW-ruh-pahds)—large plant-eating dinosaurs belonging to the saurischian group. Apatosaurus and Diplodocus are typical sauropods.

Triassic (try-ASS-ik) period—the first part of the Mesozoic era

Index

Page numbers in italic refer to illustrations.

Age of Dinosaurs, 20-21, 24-25
Allosaurus, 22, 27, 35, 57
amphibians, 24
Anatosaurus, 26
ankylosaurs, 34
Ankylosaurus, 6, 22, 26
Apatosaurus, 2, 7, 14-15, 22, 27, 42, 44, 45, 58; food of, 48-49, 56; as land animal, 10, 51, 52-53, 55, 56; as water animal, 47, 48-49
Archaeopteryx, 27

birds, 24, 25
Brachiosaurus, 2, 22, 43, 48, 52
Brontosaurus. *See* Apatosaurus

Camarasaurus, 2, 43
Coelophysis, 26
cold-blooded, 40
Cretaceous period, 25; animals of, 26-27

Diplodocus, 3, 43, 52

ectotherms, 40
eggs, dinosaur, 16, 17
endotherms, 41
environment of dinosaurs, 17; changes in, 21, 24-25
evolution of dinosaurs, 21, 22, 24-25

footprints, 16, 17, 49, 57, 59
fossils, 8-9, 16-17; formation of, 8; interpretation of, 9, 10, 12-13, 16-17

gizzards, 56

Iguanodon, 22

Jurassic period, 24-25, 28, 42, 56; animals of, 26-27

Kentrosaurus, 2, 34

Lystrosaurus, 27

Mamenchisaurus, 3, 5, 43
mammals, 24, 25
Mesozoic era, 24-25; animals of, 26-27
Monoclonius, 20

natural selection, 21

ornithischians, 21, 22
Ornitholestes, 22

paleontologists, 10, 12
Pangaea, 24
Parasaurolophus, 7, 22
Plateosaurus, 22, 26
Polacanthus, 34
Protoceratops, 20, 22
pterosaurs, 7

Quetzalcoatlus, 26

reconstruction of dinosaurs, 9, 12-13, 14-15
reptiles, 24, 25, 40, 41; dinosaurs as, 4, 24, 40, 41
Rhamphorhynchus, 6, 26

saurischians, 21, 22
sauropods, 10, 11, 42, 43, 44, 57; food of, 49, 56; lives of, 48-49, 51-53, 55
self-defense, 34, 35, 36, 37, 39, 55
skin, 17, 18-19
Stegoceras, 22
stegosaurs, 29, 33, 34
Stegosaurus, 3, 7, 22, 26, 28, 29; plates of, 28, 30-31, 32-33, 35, 36, 39, 40-41

teeth, 8, 16, 28, 49, 56
Triankeris, 27
Triassic period, 24; animals of, 26-27
Triceratops, 6, 20, 22, 27
Tuojiangosaurus, 33, 34
Tyrannosaurus, 6, 22, 26

Kunihiko Hisa created the Discovering Dinosaur books because he wanted to introduce young people to the real dinosaurs, animals that lived successfully on earth for more than 100 million years. In preparing the books, Mr. Hisa visited museums and excavations and studied the most recent discoveries of paleontologists around the world. His lively illustrations and informative texts are based on this research and on his own ideas about what dinosaurs were like and how they lived.

Sylvia A. Johnson is a writer and editor of science books for young people. In adapting the Discovering Dinosaur books for English-speaking readers, she made use not only of her scientific background but also of her experience in working with dinosaur fossils. As a volunteer in a museum laboratory, Ms. Johnson cleaned and repaired the bones of dinosaurs like Camarasaurus and Diplodocus. This first-hand experience helped her to appreciate just how "real" dinosaurs were.

This edition first published 1990 by Lerner Publications Company.
Original edition published 1982 by Akane Shobo Company, Ltd., under the title KYORYU WA DO KURASHITE ITAKA?
Text and illustrations copyright © 1982 by Kunihiko Hisa.
Additional text for this edition copyright ©1990 by Lerner Publications Company.
English translation rights arranged with Akane Shobo Company, Ltd., through Japan Foreign-Rights Centre.
Translation of original text by Wesley M. Jacobsen.

All rights to this edition reserved by Lerner Publications Company.
No part of this book may be reproduced, stored in a retrieval system, or transmitted in any form or by any means, electronic, mechanical, photocopying, recording, or otherwise, without the prior written permission of the publisher, except for the inclusion of brief quotations in an acknowledged review.

Library of Congress Cataloging-in-Publication Data

Hisa, Kunihiko. 1944-
  [Kyōryū wa dō kurashite ita ka? English]
  What were dinosaurs? / Kunihiko Hisa and Sylvia A. Johnson.
     p.   cm.
  Translation of: Kyōryū wa dō kurashite ita ka?
  Summary: Describes the evidence that modern scientists use in studying dinosaurs and the characteristics of specific dinosaurs such as Stegosaurus and Apatosaurus.
  ISBN: 0-8225-2201-2
  1. Dinosaurs—Juvenile literature. [1. Dinosaurs.] I. Johnson, Sylvia A. II. Title
QE862.D5H5813   1990
567.9'1—dc20   90-5937
                                                                  CIP
                                                                   AC

Manufactured in the United States of America
1 2 3 4 5 6 7 8 9 10 99 98 97 96 95 94 93 92 91 90